MYSTERY SHORT STORY COLLECTION VOLUME 5

CONNOR WHITELEY

No part of this book may be reproduced in any form or by any electronic or mechanical means. Including information storage, and retrieval systems, without written permission from the author except for the use of brief quotations in a book review.

This book is NOT legal, professional, medical, financial or any type of official advice.

Any questions about the book, rights licensing, or to contact the author, please email connorwhiteley@connorwhiteley.net

Copyright © 2024 CONNOR WHITELEY

All rights reserved.

DEDICATION

Thank you to all my readers without you I couldn't do what I love.

A MUMIFIED WAY TO GO

Retired Detective Kendra O'Connor had never really liked ancient, dilapidated hotels that were covered in dust, death and more cobwebs than she cared to think about. But as she sat in her favourite red leather booth in her favourite London café in the entire world, she couldn't help but think about them.

She needed the information about the hotel for a cold case as she was a member of the Cold Case Task Force, a group of retired Met police detectives that solved London's toughest, most impossible and twisted cold cases.

Kendra enjoyed the rows upon rows of little wooden tables that were lined neatly in the café. The café had changed a little in recent weeks because of a new owner so there were some weird new pieces of abstract art on the white walls that Kendra just couldn't understand.

If she wanted to look at lines of blue and red and yellow paint all day she would have painted them herself. She didn't need to buy the abstract rubbish for hundreds of pounds, it was just stupid.

The cute young male waiters in their new black uniforms were walking around confident and Kendra just couldn't believe she was admiring people that were probably more than half her age. She was so going to have to tell her husband later on, they would probably just laugh about it like they always did.

Kendra wrapped her hands around the fantastically warm mug of strong bitter coffee and she took sips of the heavenly bitterly flavour. It washed down the incredible apricot Danish pastry she had just finished perfectly. She loved the café.

Kendra watched as groups of young mothers, fathers and elderly bingo players sat on different tables on the other side of the café. They were all talking like no tomorrow, they were smiling and laughing and giggling and Kendra loved seeing other people enjoying themselves.

Especially because she knew the next cold case she was going to try and solve with her two best friends was going to make her feel pretty numb inside.

Four years ago a construction crew were stalking the halls of a nearby London hotel that had been closed for twenty years. It had been shuddered, sealed and left abandoned for twenty years until a new company brought the land and wanted to knock it all down.

Yet the crew discovered a perfectly mummified

corpse complete with bandages in one of the hotel rooms.

Kendra hated how peaceful and relaxed the young woman's body looked stretched out on the bed. Her name was Emma Oakley. There was no DNA, the woman's blood had been drained and the entire case went cold within a month. It was simply impossible to investigate a crime that theoretically occurred in a locked building.

"And that's why I don't let you drive,"

Kendra just laughed as she heard her best friend Retired Officer Patricia Nelson come into the café. She was impressed Pat was wearing black leggings, a beautiful pearl necklace and a white blouse that just somehow managed to work on her.

Kendra had always liked working with Pat, because she was amazing on computers, a brilliant person and she was just sensational to be around.

Then behind Pat was their unofficial boss of their team, retired detective Jeff Long who was wearing a soaking wet business suit with holes and tears in it. Clearly something had happened and Kendra really didn't want to know because with Jeff it could have been anything.

"What happened?" Kendra asked knowing the urge was too much.

Pat shook her head. "Jeff wanted to pick me up today because the government thinks I am too old to drive now. I let Jeff drive me so within ten minutes of leaving my house we crash,"

"We didn't crash," Jeff said. "We simply hit some pavement, drove into a black metal fence and into a small ditch in a major London park,"

Kendra just laughed.

"Then Hun," Pat said, "clever idiot over here decided he would get out the car and try and push the car out,"

"And I fell over instantly into some Stinging Nettles and branches and I ripped my suit,"

"The soaking wet part?" Kendra asked.

"Oh yeah, I went to go and get help but then a dog leapt out at me in the park, I jumped and I fell into a puddle," Jeff said.

Kendra just laughed. That was brilliant and that was such a Jeff story, it really could only happen to him of all people.

"So that's why we're late Hun," Pat said. "Any progress on the case?"

Kendra shook her head. "Original detectives were all good people I've worked with before if the case was easy then they would have solved it. The main issue is that we don't know how the killer and the victim got into the hotel in the first place. And it's wrecked now so we cannot go there,"

"Stupid judge decision to allow an active crime scene to be torn down," Jeff said.

"Hun come on, the place was deemed forensically clean by the top three forensic scientists in the country. If there was anything left in the hotel we would have found it already,"

Kendra couldn't agree more but the problem remained. So she looked at 70-something-year-old Patricia Nelson and smiled.

"You want me to bring up the blueprints don't you?" Pat asked.

Kendra nodded and watched as Pat brought out her laptop and her fingers magically danced across the keyboard. Kendra was still amazed after all this time how brilliant Pat was on the computer.

Jeff leant forward. "We need to find out what entrances for the public and for maintenance there were at the hotel,"

"Really Hun? I hadn't thought of that,"

Kendra really didn't want her two best friends to start fighting but she could understand where Pat was coming from. This always happened between her and Jeff and Jeff was just a silly idiot some of the time.

Kendra waved over a cute male waiter and asked him to bring over some napkins and more mugs of coffee so Jeff could get warm and dry himself off.

"On the blueprint there were three entrances Hun," Pat said. "It seems there was the main entrance for the public, the back entrance for staff and deliveries and an underground entrance for maintenance,"

"Okay," Kendra said. "What happened to those entrances?"

Pat spun her laptop round and brought up photos of all three entrances before, during and after being sealed up with bricks. Then there were even more photos of the entrances on the day of the discovery of the body and the day the hotel was annihilated. The entrances were still sealed up.

Kendra nodded. That wasn't what she wanted to find at all, she had wanted a break in the case but clearly this was going to be a hard problem to solve.

She took out her smartphone and dialled an old friend. "I'm calling retired Fire Chief Dawson to see if he knows anything,"

Kendra put the phone on speaker when he answered. "Hi Kendra, how are you? Hope those Cold Case lot are treating you well,"

"They are thanks," Kendra said. "You're On Speaker with Jeff Long and Patricia Nelson,"

"Hi Max," Pat said. "How's the wife and grandchildren?"

Kendra was shocked Pat actually knew the old Fire Chief for London, not a lot of people did from inside the police.

"Little Shaun went in for his final operation last week and it looks like the brain tumour's going away now so fingers cross,"

"Give him my love Hun,"

Kendra was flat out amazed Pat seemed to be really good friends with Max. It had only been lately he had mentioned to Kendra about all the health problems his youngest grandson had.

"Anyway," Jeff said, "do you remember the cold case about the mummified body in the hotel?"

"Sure do mate. That was a nasty thing to

discover, I was part of the crew on behalf of the fire department when we found her. Just nasty,"

"What ways were there to come into the building?" Jeff asked.

Kendra clicked her fingers. "Wait a minute the three main entrances were still sealed the day of the destruction. How did you get into the hotel?"

Kendra nodded her thanks to the young male waiter as he brought them all a mug of coffee each and Jeff started drying himself off.

"There's an old skylight on the roof that was unlocked. I wanted to unseal the entrances but the new owner wanted us to use the skylight," Max said.

Kendra nodded. At least that finally revealed how the killer could into the building and it was only confirmed when Pat brought up old photos of the skylight. It was massive and certainly big enough to allow several people to climb into the building without trouble.

Kendra wrapped her hands round her second wonderfully warm mug of coffee and shook her head.

"What do you mean it was unlocked?" Kendra asked.

"That's the problem," Max said over the phone. "We all thought, and the records supported this, that the entire thing would be sealed up tight including the skylight. So when we found the lock broken we couldn't find a reason for it,"

"So someone did break in and bust the lock," Jeff said.

"Yes," Max said.

"Any idea who?" Kendra asked.

"No, it seriously couldn't have been anyone and we checked the original, original blueprints before they were *updated* in London City Records and there were no extra tunnels or entrances on them,"

"Hun, what do you mean *updated*? What was removed or added to the blueprints?"

Kendra leant forward that was a brilliant point.

"That's a good point. There were three extra rooms removed over time that we double-checked and the room containing the body was one of them,"

"Did you check the other two missing rooms?" Jeff asked.

"No but the police did and there were no signs of bodies or anything amiss," Max said. "And probably sorry guys but my grandson is meant to come round in a minute. Good luck on the case and good luck with having Jeff drive you about,"

Kendra just grinned as Max hung up. She had no idea how famous or popular Jeff was in the fire department. He had clearly had a ton of friends over the years but she supposed she shouldn't be that surprised, he was a great guy.

Just not a great driver.

Kendra sat back, allowing the slight coolness of the red leather booth to claim her ageing body.

"We know she was brought in most certainly through the skylight," Kendra said. "We also know the killer most certainly came in the same way, brought in the mummification supplies and left the same way,"

"True," Jeff said finishing off his mug of coffee.

"What I don't understand is why mummify her in the first place and who would have the knowledge," Kendra asked.

Kendra watched as Pat's fingers danced across her keyboard again and again until she spun it round again and showed her something. It seemed around the time of Emma's death she was at university studying Egyptology with no boyfriend, girlfriend or any sort of romantic partner. She had a lot of friends but none of them were in the same course as her.

"Cross-reference everyone in her class with any police reports made against them," Kendra said.

"Wouldn't the original detectives have done that?" Jeff asked.

"Yes but that was four years ago. The classmates might have done something since that made them end up in a police database," Kendra said.

"Nothing Hun,"

Kendra rolled her eyes. It was worth a shot.

"What about people with a specific interest in mummification?" Kendra asked. "Maybe use one of your especially illegal programmes to check social media,"

"I do not use *illegal* computer programmes Hun, I simply use computer programmes that magically get downloaded onto my computer so the information can be obtained legally through normal channels when it comes to court,"

Kendra just nodded mockingly. She would love to see if that was a good legal defence in a court of law if Pat ever did get arrested, which Kendra just hoped beyond hope (and basically knew at this point) that no one would arrest a 70-something-year-old woman.

"Done," Pat said.

Kendra looked at the laptop and smiled as there were three people with social media pages filled with mummification posts, articles and pictures. It was a little weird but these were professional pages and the now-Masters students were clearly trying to paint themselves as early professionals in their chosen field.

Kendra looked closer as Jeff leant across the table.

The first man was a little too large, inflexible and "nerdy" by the look of his social media page to be able to basically climb and abseil down into the hotel through the skylight. He didn't seem to have any sporting interest and there was even a social media record of him arguing about the pointlessness of sports with someone.

It was a painful conversation to read.

Kendra shook her head and let Pat show her the next person.

Kendra couldn't deny this young woman was a little promising because she was President of mountain climbing, gymnastics and badminton societies at university. She was doing a lot of fitness work but when Kendra scrolled back to four years ago, she found a post mentioning the woman had shattered her right wrist in a climbing accident.

She might have been leading the societies for the past few years but she wasn't doing the sports themselves. She simply couldn't.

"Who's the last one?" Kendra asked.

Jeff shook his head and Kendra just agreed, she really wanted this lead to pan out too.

The last woman was impressive as hell as far as Kendra was concerned she graduated with a score of 98 out of 100, she was on all the sport league teams and she represented the university at national events.

"She could clearly get into the hotel, this Ruby Sofie but why would she kill Emma?" Kendra asked.

Jeff clicked his fingers. "Check something called the Academic Misconduct Dustbin,"

Kendra had no idea what that was but she watched as Pat typed it in and it turned out it was a very old government website that made universities log even small complaints of academic misconduct, like stealing. Yet unlike official university systems this one still logged the complaint even if it wasn't proven.

"Ruby was logged twice in the space of her degree Hun," Pat said. "And both times they were dropped when something bad happened to the reporting student. Emma reported Ruby for stealing her coursework the week before she died,"

"And that's our motive," Kendra said. "Question is how do we prove it?"

"Check bank account records?" Jeff asked Pat.

Pat waved him silent and she typed, swiped and pounded the keyboard a little until she just grinned.

Kendra got up out of her wonderful seat and looked at the laptop. The day before the murder Ruby ordered every single little thing she would need to mummify and kill someone and climb down into a hotel from a skylight.

She paid for it all herself, she collected the items in-person and now Kendra just wanted to see her behind bars.

"I'll call in the active detectives," Jeff said.

***

A few hours later Kendra flat out loved hanging out in her favourite café in all of London as the busy lunchtime crowd rolled in. She liked seeing all the men in their black and blue business suits and all the women in their long blouses, trousers and dresses.

They were all sitting and smiling around the little wooden table and Kendra couldn't believe how great she felt to be around so many real people again living normal everyday lives. Most of them had probably never ever heard about the murder.

The wonderful aromas of juicy roasted chicken, pork and chicken tikka sandwiches filled the air and made the fantastic taste of a curry form on her tongue. Kendra really did love this place.

Kendra loved hearing Pat and Jeff laugh with each other and they were finally getting along again now. It was great seeing them back to normal and

Kendra realised just how much she loved her retirement, because she got to do great work, solve crimes and get justice for victims. The most important thing a detective could ever wish for.

Kendra wrapped her hands round another slightly smaller mug of piping hot bitter coffee as a celebration, because Jeff had only told them moments ago Ruby had been arrested and charged for Emma's murder. She had confessed to wanting to kill Emma to get rid of the complaints against her and her cheating.

She had killed Emma after class one day and taken the body to the hotel to mummify and leave to rot. Ruby just couldn't understand why anyone would want to waste such a great learning opportunity and the experience of mummifying a corpse was the best learning she had ever done apparently.

Kendra seriously hoped Ruby was going to spend the rest of her life behind bars, and given the extreme and twisted nature of the crime, she didn't doubt that for a single moment.

And as Pat and Jeff kept on laughing, smiling and telling each other stupid stories from before their retirement, Kendra just leant across the table and joined in. These were her best friends, her family and she loved them both so much.

And she wouldn't change her life for anything. She really did love it.

FEELING ABOUT A FRAUDSTER

Private Investigator Samantha White had always loved helping others, solving crime and even volunteering at the local soup kitchen on weekends, just so she could help support her local community even more.

She even didn't mind stakeouts, which was an unfortunate but rather fun part of the private investigator life, because Samantha had managed to crack the code. She knew that a stakeout was only as boring as you made it so you always needed snacks, games and a brilliant partner to make it fun.

She sat in her small black Ford of a model she had no idea about. Samantha knew she really should brush up on her car knowledge but she had simply been too busy with doctor's appointments, solving cases and just helping people in general.

She had always liked the wonderfully warm heat of the car that was a great contrast to the sheer coldness of the winter day outside. Her entire dashboard was subtly covered in sweets, food packs and a few Tupperware containers because she knew she would be at the gym later on anyway.

Samantha kept watching the entire little narrow street. There were cute black, blue and white cars of various sizes and models lining the entire road. There were even a few ugly potholes that could have been used as a bath for most small children.

Samantha wasn't a fan of the hints of burnt petrol, burnt clutch and smoked chicken wings that left the great taste of summer picnics with Adam form on her tongue. She was looking forward to the summer again so she could have those fun dates again.

The only thing she didn't really like about the street was the ugly blue paint on the terrace houses. They were all painted the same and it just looked weird when there were front gardens of roses, vegetables and even sweetpeas that created a strange contrast.

The talking, muttering and gentle singing in someone's back garden made Samantha smile for a moment and look at beautiful Adam as he sat there in the passenger seat. Samantha had always loved his massive handsome face, his kind loving eyes and his fit sexy body.

He was so damn beautiful.

And he was always perfect to have on stakeouts because he was perfect at multi-tasking. He could just easily talk to her and focus on the target's house without ever being distracted. Samantha loved that about him.

"I don't see the target yet," Adam said, his voice wonderfully manly and sexy.

Samantha just smiled because it would be a miracle if they saw Mr Ollie Jones, considering he was meant to be claiming disability benefit from the local council, but people had claimed to have seen him walking about, laughing and even running without so much as a limp.

He was clearly committing benefit fraud but Samantha just needed to prove it with some photos. But after two days of watching carefully, Samantha was really wanting to change things up.

"What were you upset about last night?" Adam asked not daring to take his eyes off the target house.

Samantha couldn't believe he had actually noticed. She had tried so hard to cry, scream and just grieve in private without him noticing.

She couldn't tell him that she was crying because her Hormone Replacement Therapy wasn't changing her testosterone-filled body fast enough for her liking, but considering Adam had helped her from the beginning she supposed she just had to.

"I want breasts," Samantha said. "I really want to feel a physical difference and I just want to start looking like a woman. I am one on the inside, I want to be one on the outside,"

Adam nodded. "You are beautiful you know and has a client, a suspect, a police officer ever said you aren't a woman? They haven't because you are perfectly passing,"

Samantha so badly wanted to kiss him because Adam always knew just what to say and he wasn't wrong. She was glad she had always managed to pass as a woman but it was just the physical changes she wanted to hurry up but biology sadly took time.

"He isn't coming out," Adam said.

Samantha laughed. "I doubt it so we need to move onto stage two of the plan,"

"Was there a stage one?"

"Of course," Samantha said, "sit outside until we get fed up and then move on to Stage 2. Which is all about making him more likely to move without his crutches,"

Samantha loved it how Adam grinned at her, he was so cute, and she grabbed her camera and went towards Ollie Jones's house.

Samantha really liked how it was just as horrible, disgusting and tasteless as everyone else's house. It was plain awful with its blue paint, cracked windows and the front garden was simply a mess. She had no idea how many different plants were in there but there were simply too many weeds to count.

She went up to the huge window that was to the left of the wooden front door and Samantha subtly looked through the window.

She couldn't see anything of note because the damn curtains were drawn. She seriously hoped that Jones was alive and actually awake, she didn't want to get involved in a murder or death, but she did want to get inside.

Thankfully she always liked to look like a businesswoman and even despite the awfully cold temperature Samantha still made sure to wear a little black dress with black leggings. She just couldn't wear the high heels, they were death traps as far as she was concerned.

"Can I help you?" a woman asked behind her.

Samantha smiled as she looked at the short little woman in a thick black coat. She didn't look unfriendly but she hardly seemed impressed that Samantha was there.

"I am Samantha from the local Telephone provider and I was just hoping I could talk to your husband please," Samantha said.

The woman laughed. "Over my dead body is he my husband. I would much rather kill the idiot but sadly divorce is my route to freedom,"

Samantha watched the woman go over to the wooden front door and pound on it.

A few moments later a very tall and muscular man came out walking on crutches and Samantha just rolled her eyes. She had wanted Ollie Jones to slip up straight away, clearly that wasn't happening.

"What you want now Joise?" Ollie asked.

"I want you to sign the divorce papers right now," Joise said. "I am not waiting for you anymore because I don't love you,"

Samantha subtly looked back at the car and made

sure that Adam knew to film this because she really wanted to take advantage of it.

She stepped forward. "I was just curious as to why you have the curtains drawn,"

"I don't know," Ollie said grinning. "I don't want any werido looking in. Who are you?"

"I am Samantha from the local telephone company and I would like to come in and discuss your recent upgrades,"

"I don't have any upgrades," Ollie said.

"Sign the papers out here. I am not going back into that house," Joise said.

"You really should just sign the papers," Samantha said knowing that would make Ollie have to put down the crutches so he could simply sign the paperwork.

"Never," Ollie said.

Samantha shook her head. There had to be an easier way to make sure this went her way, she had to find a new way of making him move.

"What happened?" Samantha asked looking at the crutches.

"I don't know actually," Ollie said. "I was simply on the ladder at home, I slipped and fell and broke it all. I'm now done for life apparently,"

"And you have a doctor's note?" Samantha asked knowing that might be the lead she needed.

"Go away Council Scum," Ollie said.

Samantha just laughed and she walked away back towards the car because she had everything she needed. She knew that the key to proving Ollie was a fake was to find the doctor that faked all the medical reports for him.

Then she would give the doctor a simple choice. Confess and hopefully take a deal or not and the doctor would burn forever for allowing the benefit system to be ripped off.

Samantha had to find that doctor immediately.

***

After a few hours of searching online, looking through Ollie's original reports to the Council and a few more illegal searches into the world of benefit fraud, Samantha learnt that there was really only one guy everyone went to for fake medical reports. He was quick, effective and he really didn't care about ripping off local government.

He was a monster as far as Samantha was concerned.

Samantha leant on the icy cold metal of a metallic blue Nissan Leaf as she watched Doctor Noah George come towards her. She supposed the silly little car park wasn't too bad because it could only hold about ten cars but it was empty now.

It was just him and her.

There were plenty of closed, rusty shops around the car park and Samantha could see that maybe this area had been booming, filled with customers and a real slice of heaven for the locals. But that was clearly decades ago because now it was a real wasteless husk of its former self.

George frowned at Samantha as he got close. Samantha couldn't deny he looked hot in his tight blue business suit that made him look more like a banker than a medical doctor but she just wanted him to answer some questions. His looks hardly mattered.

"Who are you?" Noah asked.

"A woman who knows exactly what you do Doctor," Samantha said taking out her phone and showing him years and years' worth of medical reports that were all faked and the bank account information of ten different accounts under his name.

"What is this?" Noah asked.

"This is what you do when someone comes to you and offers you a job. People like Ollie Jones who want benefit money when they don't deserve it,"

Noah smiled. "You cannot prove this is what I do for people,"

"Really?" Samantha asked pulling up even more records on her phone. "Over two hundred people have paid you just under the legal reporting limit within two weeks of receiving their disability benefit. That is a strange thing considering how poor these people are because they are unable to work,"

Noah looked around and Samantha just sat on top of the car's bonnet.

"I am not moving and you are done for Doctor but I do have friends in the police still. They might be able to offer you a deal if you agree to give me Ollie Jones,"

"What would that involve?" Noah asked.

"You would simply have to confirm that you faked his medical reports,"

"That would destroy me,"

"That is already happening Doctor," Samantha asked.

Noah ran.

Samantha leapt off the bonnet. She hated the damn idiot. He was a dick.

Samantha chased after him.

Her feet pounding on the awfully cold path. She leapt over three cars.

She passed shops. She passed potholes.

Samantha kept running.

Noah was circling around.

He was heading back to his car.

Samantha felt something move on her chest. She ignored it.

She kept chasing Noah.

Noah took out his car keys.

Samantha hated the damn man.

He unlocked his car.

Samantha jumped through the air.

Landing by the door.

She leapt up. Opened the car door. Grabbed the steering wheel.

Noah cursed under his breath a few times and Samantha just laughed because it was time she called her police friend. They were going to have a lot of fun with this one and she just hoped beyond hope that Doctor Noah George gave her Ollie Jones so she could get paid for closing her case.

It was a long shot but she could only hope.

**

The next morning Samantha laid on top of her huge white Queen-sized bed with Adam's wonderfully topless body forming a great pillow for her head. Bright sunlight was shining in through the windows and Samantha just felt amazing about today.

The rich aromas of coffee, golden syrup and honey filled the air as Adam had decided to give her breakfast in bed, she seriously loved him and Samantha was really enjoying the silence of the apartment.

Samantha loved it as Adam started kissing her neck again and again in celebration of their little discovery last night and Samantha was so damn pleased about it. When she had been chasing Noah, the weird shaking of her chest was because her breasts had grown and Samantha couldn't believe how amazing she felt about that. The hormones were working, she was becoming who she was always meant to be and life really was wonderful.

It was the purest form of euphoria she had ever felt before and she loved it.

And Samantha was really glad when her police friend had called her about Noah George being charged with over two hundred counts of Fraud. The police were certainly going to be busy and her friend had agreed to pass on the information to her today so she could present it to the Council and she could get paid.

Samantha was so going to ask for a heavier fee after discovering just how extreme the fraud went, but that was why she did what she did. She loved her job because she got to solve crime, help people and now so many families that needed the benefit system were going to get more money because less of it was leaking away because of fraud.

She knew that benefit fraud was rare as hell but she hated it when she discovered it because it really wasn't a victimless crime. And she was really glad that Noah George, Ollie Jones and so many others were going to go away for a long, long time.

And that was all because she had had a feeling about the fraudster and trusted herself.

DARK DEPENDENCY

Recovered diary entrances of convicted killer Bobby Crank.

***

8th August 2023

Dear Diary,

I was never normally this hurt, upset and pained by the sheer state of the world, because you very well know I am an excellent person. I normally spend tonight at the soup kitchen talking to the homeless people, I also read to the elderly on weekends and most importantly I support the sweet little kids at that excuse of a school down my road.

I wasn't a bad person and I really do love life. I am not intense, insane or simply deranged.

I will tell you though and prove it to you that I am none of those awful, hurt things. Since I am currently lying in my nice warm bed, the softness of the cotton-scented fabric covers my body gently and lovingly. The fabric isn't too warm nor cool, it is just right.

The great taste of apple pie still lingers in my mouth from the great dessert I had when I was out with friends only a few hours earlier. And my bedroom is as bright, colourful and welcoming as always.

I mean how else is a university student's bedroom meant to look, except welcoming?

I would never be able to get a girl back to my bedroom for some adult fun if it wasn't the best it could possibly be, right? It's why the walls are sterile white, cold and wonderful pictures of my holidays and other travels cover them. From France to Spain to Canada and everything in-between the walls clearly show I am interesting, lovely and I am not insane at all.

Of course there are tons of textbooks on murder, blood and police investigations but I am a policing student, so surely no one can ever hold such things against little old me?

Anyway, my dearest diary I am afraid I am letting myself go yet again. I need to tell you that at the amazing dinner with my friends we were all laughing, smiling and talking about everything and nothing like we always did.

Joe was being a bit of a player and telling us about his sexual conquests. He looked rather nice in his brown shirt and tight black jeans that, according to his girlfriend Aleshia, always left little to the imagination. I had always liked hanging out with Joe because he was just a wonderful person to have around.

Aleshia herself was hot and sexy as always. Her little black dress was perfectly seductive and I loved hearing about her coursework project to do with physics and a bunch of other things I simply didn't understand.

And dear, dear Everliegh was beautiful as ever. She was so cute, sweet and innocent-looking. She might have gotten a new boyfriend yesterday and I wanted her and I was going to get her, I simply wasn't allowing some other man to get what was mine.

Everleigh belonged to me and that was final.

But it turns out that when I said words to that effect to Everleigh she claimed that I was insane, crazy and I needed professional help. I simply couldn't believe she had met her boyfriend a single day before and he had always turned her against me.

I tried to explain myself but poor Everleigh had been too corrupted and she was past the point of no return.

She still wanted to be friends but she needed a little bit of space. She claimed that space would be great for us and for me to understand that friendship was deadly important, and I would in the end care more about her as a friend and not as a potential romantic partner.

I just smiled, nodded and waved her goodnight because she was wrong about everything but she was right about being deadly important to me.

I wanted to try to give her space but I simply couldn't allow her out of my life.

***

10th August 2023

Diary, I am dying here.

I cannot do this any longer. My chest feels so tight, sweat is pouring down my back and my stomach fills like it is about to explode at any moment.

Even the entire world seems twisted, strange and warped against me somehow. I am still lying in my bed but the normally soft, silky, smooth sheets feel like fire ants are crawling all over me. They want to hurt me, kill me and they want me to suffer.

My bedsheets might have smelt like sweet cotton for the past few nights but tonight they seriously don't. They stink of horrible coffee that makes the foul taste of walnut and coffee cake form on my tongue. I hated the same cake when my grandmother used to make it, and I hate it even more now.

There's even a party across the road with loud screams, awful songs and people shouting at each other. I cannot think clearly and it is like the entire world is trying to punish me.

I cannot do this without Everleigh anymore, I have to contact her, I have to talk to her. I have to be with her.

I cannot describe the headache corkscrewing across my skull but it is getting louder and louder. I just feel like I am dying without her and I have spoken to some mental health crappers and they assure me this is simply emotional dependency, but I know they are liars.

This is love, dedication and admiration. I will have Everleigh even if I have to kill that dumb boyfriend of hers forever.

Yes. Yes.

Maybe that is exactly what I need to do diary, maybe I need to save and rescue Everleigh from the evil, corrupter that is her boyfriend. Then she would always be grateful to me and she would want to be with me forever. She could finally be my wife and that would be sensational.

Goodbye sweet diary because I have to start planning now.

***

14th August 2023

Diary, I did it all. The corrupter is dead and now I will be free forever.

I guess I should start at the beginning because that is the least that you, my dear friend, deserve for helping, supporting and urging me on all this time.

The plan was really simple actually and it only got simpler as I sat in my cold little black Kia car. The fabric seats were as holey, damp and icy cold as always and the entire car stunk of cigarettes because my brother had borrowed it earlier that day.

The foul taste of tobacco formed on my tongue and I hated my brother even more. How dare he force me to endure that disgusting habit of his and he wasn't even here to suffer with me, even though I doubt it would be suffering for him.

I was parked on a narrow little road with large terrace houses lining the street. There were a lot of young families, a lot of happy schoolchildren walking up and down the road and my target's house was simple enough to find.

Everleigh's evil boyfriend was called Scott Barker, a jock at the local university and his awful curly black hair was so disgusting that I wanted to shave his head before killing him.

His house was no different to the rest of the street. All the houses had the same white painted exterior, the same red and yellow brick driveaway and the exact same blue door. The only reason I knew why Scott lived where he did was because of the house number, and I had noticed the house number on a few photos on social media.

He was hardly difficult to track down.

So I did what any sane person would do and I watched the house for four consecutive nights, I watched his routines and I realised that Scott always walked home at 7 pm alone, he didn't talk to someone on the phone or walk a dog. It was just him.

And it was just him on the street and thankfully this wasn't one of those weird streets where someone was constantly looking out the windows and making notes.

There weren't even any doorbell cameras so I could happily kill him without anyone seeing me.

And that's what I did.

It was the fourth night and I had parked in a different place tonight where I knew Scott always passed as he walked home. I had a massive knife that belonged to my father from his hunting days and I just waited for Scott to walk past.

Thankfully I didn't have to wait too long and my entire body filled with such beautiful relief that sooner or later I could finally be with my love again. Soon Everleigh would come running back to me and I could simply love her, comfort her and be with her forever.

I watched Scott walk past my car, he didn't see me, and I just hated him more with each passing moment. He had his little black gym bag and the sweat was still rolling down his back.

He was a disgusting jock that didn't deserve someone like Everleigh because she was innocent, he was not.

It was why he had to die.

So I got out the car and I simply slit his throat and enjoyed the amazingly wonderful thud as his corpse hit the ground.

Everleigh was one step closer to being mine.

***

16th August 2023

Dear Diary,

People have to be the most ungrateful creatures ever to walk this damn earth. I told Everleigh that she was now free, she could be happy and she could fall in love with me without the evil Scott controlling her thinking. And you know what? She of all people was actually scared of me, me of all people!

I have just saved her from a life of control, abuse and torment and the damn woman doesn't even have the respect to say thank you. I mean, I have just killed a bloody jock for her and she didn't say thank you. She was evil, twisted and it was just typical that Scott's foul control was still impacting our relationship.

Maybe I should have acted sooner. Maybe I should have gathered more evidence on how abusive and controlling Scott was towards Everleigh so I could reveal the extent of it to Everleigh. Maybe I should have done a lot of things differently.

Not that it matters now.

Poor, dumb little Everleigh called the cops on me and now I am in my little grey metal prison cell. The walls are horrible and grey like my mood. I really don't like the ceiling very much because it is made from the same horrible grey blocks that my grandmother's house was made from. I hated the house then and I hate it even more now.

The entire damn prison cell smells of poo, urine and sweat because the metal prison toilet doesn't work half the time. It's useless, just like Everleigh and Scott and all my other former friends.

I couldn't believe that they believed Everleigh over me when they said I was crazy, deranged and intense. This was all their fault and now I realise Everleigh will never ever be mine.

But maybe that is okay because I will be moved tomorrow from my prison cell at this county prison and moved up North towards a larger, better prison with psychological facilities to treat me.

Yet I need no treatment because I feel the best I have in years because my aim, my purpose and my sole dedication in life has been revealed to me. I will hunt down my former friends, I will hunt down Everleigh and I will hunt down everyone who made me end up in prison.

And I will kill them all.

I couldn't help but grin to myself because that really was a beautiful, beautiful idea. And it gave me such wonderful hope for a better future for everyone involved.

**

1st September 2023

Bobby Crank was killed by Armed Tactical Response Officers when he escaped and tried to kill Everleigh and a group of his former friends.

ATTEMPTED BURNING

The thick rich aroma of smoke, burning rubber and burnt hair woke Judith Mitchel immediately. Her eyes opened. She didn't struggle, that would waste precious oxygen. Her experience kicked in.

Later Judith would question why her killer didn't just shoot her as she slept on the pile of hay. It wouldn't have been hard. It would have been far too easy in all honesty.

The loud cracking and roaring of the bright red and yellow and orange flames raced up the wooden sides of the barn. Paint burnt away quickly. Immense wooden beams were devoured and chomped away by the flames.

Judith got up immediately covering her mouth and nose with her loose t-shirt. She had to escape. She couldn't see anything except smoke and flames.

She felt a draft coming from behind her so she ran towards it. Boiling hot flames licked her skin. She kept running and jumping over flames and burning timber.

Moments later the sheer icy coldness of the outside air met her and Judith forced herself to keep going until she was a fair distance away from the ablaze barn. She had no idea how she had gotten there but she didn't care.

Judith simply focused on her deep breathing and wanting to enjoy the sweet mint-scented air as the grass and mint under her feet was crushed. A great reminder of childhood as the taste of mint ice cream formed on her tongue.

Judith scanned the area and as much as she wanted to focus on the immense woodland around the circular clearing. She could only focus on the burning barn in the middle.

She had no idea what colour it might have once been. The paint and even a lot of the timber had been burnt away or collapsed in on itself. The roaring, howling, deafening flames kept devouring the barn like a child wanting their favourite dinner.

Someone had wanted her dead. That much was obvious but Judith couldn't understand who. She was going out with friends and was about to meet them then everything had gone black.

A lot of her memory was a blur but she shivered as the icy coldness of the light wind picked up. If the killer was close and watching the barn then Judith didn't doubt they would know she was alive.

Judith had to get moving but her experience taught her there were limited options even in that.

The few advantages of being a police fugitive tracker.

Not that the chance of getting hunted down on the road or being hunted through the woodland was actually going to stop her.

A loud explosion ripped through the clearing as something inside the barn went off.

Judith shook her head and went away from the barn. It was stupid to stay at the barn for so long. She should have been in the woodlands already.

It was a stupid mistake. One that Judith really hoped wouldn't cost her her life.

A bullet screamed towards her.

Heat rushed past her head.

Judith ran towards the trees.

Dirt exploded in front of her.

She dived to one side.

More bullets screamed towards her.

Agony shot up her right leg as a bullet smashed into it.

She collapsed to the ground.

Judith made sure to stay down in case the killer wanted to try again. She couldn't die. She couldn't do anything.

Judith heard heavy footsteps crush the ground unleashing more minty goodness in the air and she still didn't turn to see who was coming towards her. It had to be her killer that much was obvious.

"I thought you would be a little harder to kill,"

Judith's eyes widened as she recognised the voice, the movement and the slight charm in the voice. Her boss was here. Judith had flat out no idea why her boss wanted her dead or was daring to do this at all but she wanted answers.

And she wanted to live.

Judith slowly moved her head in an effort not to scare him or make him believe she was a threat, for now. Judith's best choice might have been to play along but she really wanted to get her hands on that damn gun.

Then she saw her boss and her stomach twisted into an agonising knot. Judith had to admit he looked good in his red chequered shirt, blue jeans and short blond hair. He looked really good.

But there was a strange hunger, a strange derangement and a strange everything in his eyes. Judith had never seen the hunger on him, she had seen it on serial killers and the various scumbags she hunted for her job but never her boss.

"Why?" Judith asked hating how scared her sounded.

"Because," her boss said grinning, "I hate you. You capture more fugitives than anyone else and there is talk you know in the station,"

Judith shrugged and her eyes focused on the large rifle in his hands. She had been hoping for a little handgun but rifles were a lot harder to simply grab off someone.

"They want you to become the Head of Fugitive Taskforce. They want you to replace me because apparently I am no longer good at my job,"

"You could simply try to get rid of me at work. You could try to sack me or discredit me. Why try to kill me?"

Judith hated it how her boss's eyes lit up and reflected the intensity of the fire perfectly.

"Because it's been six months since I killed something. Normally I like killing homeless people or sex workers but well… you were simply the more delightful option,"

Judith sat up and hissed in pain as she accidentally placed a little too much pressure on her right leg.

Her boss held out the rifle.

"How many?" Judith asked wanting to buy herself more time. She had managed to disarm a man with a rifle before by getting close enough to him to do some sort of attack.

She needed to buy herself more time and then she could hopefully do the same to him.

"I don't know," her boss said. "I kill every 6 months like clockwork,"

"Wait," Judith said hating she hadn't realised this sooner, "every 6 months you go on holiday with your wife. The wife we have never met,"

Her boss grinned. "Oh so you have finally figured it out. If I was being honest I suppose I should say they're my *Killing Holidays* or maybe even *Hunting Trips*,"

Judith forced herself to grin as her boss came a little closer to her so Judith pretended to hiss out in agony and fall down.

Her boss came even closer to her and Judith noticed that some of the hunger and intensity in his eyes were dying out now. Maybe he just wanted to confess to someone but if he was willing to burn her alive in the barn then Judith knew he would kill her at a moment's notice.

Judith smiled as her boss's shoes touched hers.

She threw herself forward. The roaring flames died down in the distance.

She grabbed the rifle.

Her boss hissed.

Judith threw her weight to one side.

The rifle went with her.

Her boss let go. He kicked her. Punched her.

Judith went to aim the rifle. He was too close.

He grabbed the other end.

Judith kicked him with her right leg. She screamed in agony.

Her boss took the rifle back.

"You are nothing but a stupid cop," he said.

Judith just stared at him as she realised that she really had made a mistake. She should have gone to the gym more maybe if she had done that she'd be tougher, stronger, more capable.

Her boss grinned. "I like watching people break before I kill them."

Judith shook her head and she realised for the first time that this was always how killers worked and killers were caught. Killers fed off someone's fears, desperation and utter helplessness but Judith wasn't helpless.

She was a cop first and foremost and she had survived a lot more hunt for fugitives than she felt like she deserved.

And she was going to survive this.

"Look at your beautiful work behind you," Judith said.

Her boss turned around so his back was to her and Judith kicked him in the back of the knees.

Pure agony shot through her. She climbed forward.

Climbing on top of her boss. He tried to move. She didn't let him.

She punched him in the back of the head.

He let go of the rifle.

Judith grabbed it. Whacking him over the back of the head.

His skull cracked.

The roaring flames in the distance died down even more.

Judith pushed his face into the soft minty grass. She pressed down with all her strength.

She felt him tense. Kick. Try to punch.

But it was all useless as after two minutes he really did stop moving and Judith whacked him over the back of the head again for good measure.

Judith stood up with the rifle still firmly in her hand and she shot him in the right leg just in case he was alive. And then she slowly started dragging him towards the barn. She didn't know why she wanted to burn the body but she really, really did.

She could understand why her boss had been so desperate to protect himself that he had tried to kill her. She had seen a lot of people kill for a lot less but she really needed to make sure he could never hurt another person.

Of course there would be questions and she would have to answer them. But she didn't doubt that as soon as the police got a warrant for her boss's home Judith had no doubt they would find a lot of horrors to explain her version of events and how he had "accidentally" fell into the burning barn.

Judith pushed the body onto the burning barn and felt a little relief as the body didn't move or jerk as the flames engulfed it. At least he wasn't alive and he wasn't going to suffer anymore.

She stayed there for another ten minutes until the body was nice and toasty and cooked and then she simply went away. She went through the forest to a nearby town, called for help and everything went perfectly from there.

Over forty cold cases were solved because her boss used to kill every three months instead of six. A lot of families were pleased and Judith was hailed a hero and even better she was now the head of the Fugitive Taskforce.

And she really couldn't help but wonder if her boss hadn't tried to kill her, would she have taken the job? She wasn't sure at all but she flat out loved her new life, her new job and her new amazing team. Something that was only possible because her boss had attempted to burn her alive.

FINDING SARAH

Private Investigator Leo Ashley just shook their head as they looked at the massive flowery display Sarah, their personal assistant, had done them on the massive ancient oak desk that covered half the office. Leo had always liked the office more than they cared to admit.

It was their little slice of heaven and a safe beacon whenever they weren't investigating a case, saving lives or simply doing stakeouts. Leo wasn't a massive fan of stakeouts but clients loved to pay the bills so it was worth it.

And it was always worth it to see the happy, smiling face of a client. Leo really did love being a private investigator.

There wasn't actually a lot to dislike about the office. Leo had always liked its large square design, with a small kitchenette in one tiny corner where they could make their morning coffee and afternoon tea. Leo had always enjoyed the bright warming sunlight that shone through the floor-to-ceiling windows that made the office seem classy, modern and like they were a well-to-do private investigator.

But as Leo just looked at the massive flowery display that covered the entirety of their desk. And made the entire office stink of lavender, roses and lilacs, Leo really wasn't impressed and this just wasn't normal.

Sarah had always mentioned that she loved flowers, Leo understood it and whenever they needed a flower opinion on a case. Leo had always gone to her because she was the expert but this was just flat out weird.

The rest of the office building was silent and Leo really wanted to know where their assistant was. Sarah was normally always on time, she was always dressed smart and she had never made a mess before.

Leo supposed they couldn't be too angry. Sarah might have been busy last night, Leo always let her use the office space for whatever she wanted. They normally allowed her to paint, do crafts and even host dinner dates in the conference room for all her friends, because it was the nice thing to do.

But Sarah wasn't here and that was seriously starting to concern Leo more than they ever wanted to admit.

They went over to the heavily-scented desk that made Leo want to cough more and more. They might have been non-binary but they could see the card written out on top perfectly. It was a small white card with black writing on it clearly in Sarah's handwriting.

It read *it doesn't matter about the child. I will still love it.*

Leo just grinned. They and their wife had been telling all their friends lately and everyone important to them that they were going to raise the kid gender-neutral until they were old enough to decide for themselves. Leo didn't mind that and if the kid wanted to be a boy, girl or whatever then they were going to support them no matter what.

It wasn't gender that made a kid a great person, it was the love, support and affection that was given to them. And Leo was going to love their kid so damn much.

Sarah still wasn't here.

Leo took out their phone and dialled Sarah.

A moment later a loud ring echoed across the entire office and Leo realised the ring was actually coming from the desk itself.

They managed to search the desk and Leo found under a small pile of roses, Sarah's black phone was still turned on, ringing and no one else had phoned her.

Leo couldn't believe that Sarah was missing. She was such an amazing person, such a great worker and she was so damn popular. Leo was still amazed even after working with her for ten years how popular she was, they could be walking down the street and ten people could ask how she was these days.

Sarah lived on her phone and Leo doubted she

even knew how to turn it off. Sarah was just never ever off the bloody thing.

Leo just bit their lower lip as they realised that Sarah really was in trouble and this wasn't a joke, it wasn't her trying to be harsh or anything like that.

She was actually in trouble and she needed his help, now.

Leo was tempted to call the police but they realised the flowers had to be the key. Leo had seen Sarah like and pick and bring in a lot of flowers before but never roses or lavender.

Leo actually doubted Sarah even liked lavender. It was such a strong awful smell and Sarah had always liked sweet and more subtle tones. Lavender was just way, way too strong for her and that meant the kidnapper (and hopefully not killer) had brought them in.

Leo carefully searched through the flowers to see if the kidnapper hadn't taken off the tags. Maybe there was still a sign of the kidnapper, a piece of forensic evidence or anything else that the kidnapper might have left behind.

There was nothing.

Leo had searched through every single flower when they realised each one was perfectly (almost forensically) clean and that was a mistake and rather revealing in itself.

Leo went over to the floor-to-ceiling windows and looked down at the wide cobblestone street below and tens upon tens of ancient masonry buildings lining it. The kidnapper hadn't been normal and just grabbed a bunch of flowers and laid them out on the table.

They had been careful, cleaned them and made sure not a single flower could be traced back to them. That meant the kidnapper had been planning this for days, maybe even weeks or months and that meant Sarah was targeted.

Or maybe Leo was being targeted and Sarah was being held hostage so someone could get to them.

Leo shook their head as they knew of only one single person on this Earth that would be evil enough to do such a thing.

Their father.

Leo had never liked their father. He was harsh, evil and extremely backwards about the state of the world and trans rights, but that wasn't what this was about.

Leo hated how their father had hated Sarah from the moment Leo had mentioned she was working for him. Their father had just never understood why a woman would be working in a male-dominated world.

Their father had always believed that women shouldn't be investigators or assistants. They should simply be stuck in the kitchen and hurt if they left.

Leo grabbed their car keys because they had to see their father and Leo wasn't leaving without Sarah.

No matter what it took.

***

About an hour later, Leo slowly drove up along

the black gravel driveway towards their father's little cottage. Leo had always liked how the yellow stone blocks of the cottage were weathered, chipped and looked like they had stood for a thousand years without collapsing. It was often how they described themselves, they had endured a lot of trauma and abuse over the years.

But now Leo was finally their true self and that was simply amazing.

Leo noticed movement at the bottom window and a grumpy ancient face was frowning back. There was a massive black SUV parked in one corner and Leo had no intention of allowing their father to escape so they parked in front of it.

Leo got out the car and was surprised at the sheer amount of damp, smoke and charred wood in the air. Their father was clearly having a house inside and maybe he was right too. The dark grey sky was hardly that inspiring but Leo just wanted to get Sarah and leave.

They went over to the massive brown front door and knocked on it. The deafening pounding echoed through the entire house and Leo wanted to punch their father for daring to do this.

A moment later their father opened the door, and their father laughed at him. Leo hated how their father looked with his awful frown lines, cardigan that didn't fit him and he looked like a wreck. Leo had tried to help him over the years but their father was just foul.

Leo really did support why their mother had divorced the old bastard. Their mother just wanted to be happy with her life, and Leo understood that feeling all too well.

"What do you want *man*?" their father asked.

Leo smiled because they had always hated how their father had used that single word like a sword against them. This wasn't the time for correction though, Leo knew who they were and that was all that mattered.

"Where's Sarah?" Leo asked. "I know you took her and now I want you to free her,"

Their father smiled. "That little woman never should have worked for you. She was a left-winger and she supported your deluded crap. You are a man and you have to accept that or I will kill everyone who supports that crap,"

Leo just looked at their father. They couldn't, just couldn't believe that Sarah was dead because she was trying to be a good person, a good human being and the bestest friend he ever could have asked for.

"Get out," their father said.

Leo pushed past him and went through a horrible dirty corridor and went into a massive living room. The sheer aroma of urine was choking and overwhelming, Leo hated it but they had never ever suspected to see Sarah just sitting there with a cup of coffee.

Leo just stared at Sarah with her long brown hair, perfect body and beautifully innocent eyes that were a strange mixture of fear and thanks for seeing them. Leo didn't understand what was happening but they wanted to find out so badly.

The cold metal of a blade against their back made Leo realise that wasn't happening peacefully.

"I was just getting to know my little house guest," their father said placing Leo in a headlock. "I was just seeing what she liked, disliked and we were planning a life together,"

"He's crazy," Sarah said. "He took me, threatened to kill you if I didn't go,"

"That's what a good woman does-"

"Enough," Leo said knowing their father was about to say something extremely sexist.

"I don't want to hear another word out of you," Leo said.

"What's wrong *man?* Don't you know when you can't win a situation or a situation *boy?*"

Leo shook their head because Sarah was safe, their father had confessed to kidnapping and Leo understood that everything was going to be okay if they could simply get the knife away.

"What if I told you Mum's coming?" Leo asked.

"Liar," their father said, his voice unstable.

"No really. It's why I came early and tried to call you ten times. You know how bad you are on the phone. I tried and tried to call,"

Leo felt the icy coldness of the blade become less intense so maybe their father had taken it away slightly.

"I don't believe you *man*,"

Leo sighed. "I didn't want to say this but Mum's got some new black bras with lacey finishes,"

Leo forced themselves not to smile as their father took the knife away and went over to the window.

Leo charged.

They leapt through the air.

Tackling their father to the ground.

The father kicked.

Punched.

Fought back.

Leo whacked their father.

Sarah shot up.

She stomped on the knife.

Leo knocked out their father.

And Leo just looked at their wonderfully resourceful, clever and brilliant assistant now that she was perfectly safe.

"Sarah, can you please call the police?" Leo asked more concerned on making sure their father didn't escape.

***

A few hours later Leo and Sarah were both standing in front of the immense floor-to-ceiling windows looking at the bright blue sky outside with hundreds of little sparrows swirling, twirling and whirling around each other. There were tons of little old ladies and men in their cardigans doing some shopping on the cobblestone street and everything really was right with the world.

Leo really loved it how their father had been arrested, charged and Sarah was never going to have to see him ever again. Leo was just glad she was okay and happy with how everything had turned out.

She didn't want to go home alone for a little while and Leo just hugged her. They understood that feeling after trauma so they would always support her but if she was scared to be alone for too long then Leo would pay for her to see a therapist, because they were basically magic in their experience.

Leo liked it even more that the office no longer stunk of roses, lavender and lilacs. Leo still couldn't understand their father had simply added the flowers to make Leo panic more about their dear friend, Leo was so glad they would never have to see their father ever again.

Their father was simply toxic.

"Did you want to stay with me and Beth tonight?" Leo asked really hoping she would say yes. "You can see the baby and they are so cute these days,"

"I would actually love that after today thanks," Sarah said knowing they wanted her to say yes. "I do just have one small question for you though, what do I call the baby?"

Leo laughed and hugged her and even gave her a little kiss on the cheek. Sarah really was amazing because she had been kidnapped by their father, forced to actually talk to him (a torture in itself) and she still actually cared more about what to call a baby than herself.

"Just call Emily by their name," Leo said and as them and Sarah left the office, Leo made sure to lock it extra tight tonight because they didn't want anyone else going inside and gifting them awful flowers.

And then they both went home and had a wonderful night filled with laughter, friendship and a lot of baby cuddling. The very best definition of a perfect night with a perfect friend and an amazing wife too.

GET YOUR FREE SHORT STORY NOW!
And get signed up to Connor Whiteley's newsletter to hear about new gripping books, offers and exciting projects. (You'll never be sent spam)

https://www.subscribepage.io/wintersignup

About the author:

Connor Whiteley is the author of over 60 books in the sci-fi fantasy, nonfiction psychology and books for writer's genre and he is a Human Branding Speaker and Consultant.

He is a passionate warhammer 40,000 reader, psychology student and author.

Who narrates his own audiobooks and he hosts The Psychology World Podcast.

All whilst studying Psychology at the University of Kent, England.

Also, he was a former Explorer Scout where he gave a speech to the Maltese President in August 2018 and he attended Prince Charles' 70th Birthday Party at Buckingham Palace in May 2018.

Plus, he is a self-confessed coffee lover!

<u>Other books by Connor Whiteley:</u>
<u>Bettie English Private Eye Series</u>
A Very Private Woman
The Russian Case
A Very Urgent Matter
A Case Most Personal
Trains, Scots and Private Eyes
The Federation Protects
Cops, Robbers and Private Eyes
Just Ask Bettie English
An Inheritance To Die For
The Death of Graham Adams
Bearing Witness
The Twelve
The Wrong Body
The Assassination Of Bettie English
Wining And Dying
Eight Hours
Uniformed Cabal
A Case Most Christmas

<u>Gay Romance Novellas</u>
Breaking, Nursing, Repairing A Broken Heart
Jacob And Daniel
Fallen For A Lie
Spying And Weddings
Clean Break

MYSTERY SHORT STORY COLLECTION VOLUME 5

Awakening Love
Meeting A Country Man
Loving Prime Minister
Snowed In Love
Never Been Kissed
Love Betrays You

<u>Lord of War Origin Trilogy:</u>
Not Scared Of The Dark
Madness
Burn Them All

<u>The Fireheart Fantasy Series</u>
Heart of Fire
Heart of Lies
Heart of Prophecy
Heart of Bones
Heart of Fate

<u>City of Assassins (Urban Fantasy)</u>
City of Death
City of Martyrs
City of Pleasure
City of Power

Agents of The Emperor
Return of The Ancient Ones
Vigilance
Angels of Fire
Kingmaker
The Eight
The Lost Generation
Hunt
Emperor's Council
Speaker of Treachery
Birth Of The Empire
Terraforma
Spaceguard

The Rising Augusta Fantasy Adventure Series
Rise To Power
Rising Walls
Rising Force
Rising Realm

Lord Of War Trilogy (Agents of The Emperor)
Not Scared Of The Dark
Madness
Burn It All Down

MYSTERY SHORT STORY COLLECTION VOLUME 5

Miscellaneous:
RETURN
FREEDOM
SALVATION
Reflection of Mount Flame
The Masked One
The Great Deer
English Independence

OTHER SHORT STORIES BY CONNOR WHITELEY

Mystery Short Story Collections
Criminally Good Stories Volume 1: 20 Detective Mystery Short Stories
Criminally Good Stories Volume 2: 20 Private Investigator Short Stories
Criminally Good Stories Volume 3: 20 Crime Fiction Short Stories
Criminally Good Stories Volume 4: 20 Science Fiction and Fantasy Mystery Short Stories
Criminally Good Stories Volume 5: 20 Romantic Suspense Short Stories

Mystery Short Stories:
Protecting The Woman She Hated
Finding A Royal Friend

Our Woman In Paris
Corrupt Driving
A Prime Assassination
Jubilee Thief
Jubilee, Terror, Celebrations
Negative Jubilation
Ghostly Jubilation
Killing For Womenkind
A Snowy Death
Miracle Of Death
A Spy In Rome
The 12:30 To St Pancreas
A Country In Trouble
A Smokey Way To Go
A Spicy Way To GO
A Marketing Way To Go
A Missing Way To Go
A Showering Way To Go
Poison In The Candy Cane
Kendra Detective Mystery Collection Volume 1
Kendra Detective Mystery Collection Volume 2
Mystery Short Story Collection Volume 1
Mystery Short Story Collection Volume 2
Criminal Performance
Candy Detectives

MYSTERY SHORT STORY COLLECTION VOLUME 5

Key To Birth In The Past

<u>Science Fiction Short Stories:</u>
Their Brave New World
Gummy Bear Detective
The Candy Detective
What Candies Fear
The Blurred Image
Shattered Legions
The First Rememberer
Life of A Rememberer
System of Wonder
Lifesaver
Remarkable Way She Died
The Interrogation of Annabella Stormic
Blade of The Emperor
Arbiter's Truth
Computation of Battle
Old One's Wrath
Puppets and Masters
Ship of Plague
Interrogation
Edge of Failure

<u>Fantasy Short Stories:</u>
City of Snow
City of Light
City of Vengeance
Dragons, Goats and Kingdom
Smog The Pathetic Dragon
Don't Go In The Shed
The Tomato Saver
The Remarkable Way She Died
Dragon Coins
Dragon Tea
Dragon Rider

<u>All books in 'An Introductory Series':</u>
Clinical Psychology and Transgender Clients
Clinical Psychology
Careers In Psychology
Psychology of Suicide
Dementia Psychology
Clinical Psychology Reflections Volume 4
Forensic Psychology of Terrorism And Hostage-Taking
Forensic Psychology of False Allegations
Year In Psychology
CBT For Anxiety
CBT For Depression
Applied Psychology

MYSTERY SHORT STORY COLLECTION VOLUME 5

BIOLOGICAL PSYCHOLOGY 3RD EDITION
COGNITIVE PSYCHOLOGY THIRD EDITION
SOCIAL PSYCHOLOGY- 3RD EDITION
ABNORMAL PSYCHOLOGY 3RD EDITION
PSYCHOLOGY OF RELATIONSHIPS- 3RD EDITION
DEVELOPMENTAL PSYCHOLOGY 3RD EDITION
HEALTH PSYCHOLOGY
RESEARCH IN PSYCHOLOGY
A GUIDE TO MENTAL HEALTH AND TREATMENT AROUND THE WORLD- A GLOBAL LOOK AT DEPRESSION
FORENSIC PSYCHOLOGY
THE FORENSIC PSYCHOLOGY OF THEFT, BURGLARY AND OTHER CRIMES AGAINST PROPERTY
CRIMINAL PROFILING: A FORENSIC PSYCHOLOGY GUIDE TO FBI PROFILING AND GEOGRAPHICAL AND STATISTICAL PROFILING.
CLINICAL PSYCHOLOGY
FORMULATION IN PSYCHOTHERAPY
PERSONALITY PSYCHOLOGY AND

INDIVIDUAL DIFFERENCES
CLINICAL PSYCHOLOGY REFLECTIONS VOLUME 1
CLINICAL PSYCHOLOGY REFLECTIONS VOLUME 2
Clinical Psychology Reflections Volume 3
CULT PSYCHOLOGY
Police Psychology

A Psychology Student's Guide To University
How Does University Work?
A Student's Guide To University And Learning
University Mental Health and Mindset

www.ingramcontent.com/pod-product-compliance
Lightning Source LLC
LaVergne TN
LVHW012127070526
838202LV00056B/5905